Santa Baby

Smriti Prasadam-Halls

Ada Grey

BLOOMSBURY
LONDON OXFORD NEW YORK NEW DELHI SYDNEY

'Twas Christmas Eve and Santa Claus pulled on his Santa suit.
He filled his sack with presents, and shone his big black boots.
He saddled up his reindeer, and polished up his sleigh.
"Now everything is set!" he said, "I must be on my way."

Santa Baby hopped about –
he wanted to go too.
He tried to sneak aboard the sleigh
but Santa somehow knew.

"You're far too young to come along, you know that," Santa said.
"And you'll only get your presents if you're tucked up tight in bed."

"It's so unfair!" moaned Santa Baby to his best friend Roo
- who'd heard from Daddy Reindeer that he had to stay home, too.

"It's boring!" Roo sighed grumpily. "It's just no fun at all.
They always tell us we can't go because of being small."

"Now off to bed," said Santa,
as he kissed them both goodbye.
Then – before you could say "Christmas"
– he'd sped off into the sky.

Poor Roo and Santa Baby watched the sleigh fly out of sight.
"We're missing out again," they sighed, "for yet *another* night."

But when the two friends stepped indoors,
do you know what they saw?
Two brightly coloured parcels,
hidden just behind the door!

"Oh, no! Dad's left some gifts behind,
I bet he doesn't know!
Hey Roo, let's try to catch him up.
Come quick! We have to go . . .

. . . for if we don't, a boy or girl will wake up feeling sad.
They'll think they've been forgotten
or they'll think that they've been bad."

They smiled at one another as they ran out to their sleigh.
And taking to the skies they cried,
"We're off to save the day!"

The friends were so excited as they soared into the night,
but soon their elf friends stopped them . . .

for a super snowball fight!

Splat!

Splot!

Squelch!

The snowballs squelched and splatted
but it wasn't long before . . .
they had to wave goodbye and
then be on their way once more.

They sped across the mountains on their sparkly starlit ride,
but then some penguins stopped them . . .

for a super slippy slide!

Whee!

Whizz!

Whoosh!

They slipped and slid and whooshed and whizzed
beneath the big bright moon.
But – "We have to go!" said Santa Baby,
"Morning will come soon!"

At last they spotted rooftops and they started swooping low,
the chimneys, trees and fairy lights all sparkled in the snow.

"You know what we should do?" said Santa Baby, with a whoop . . .
"Let's gallop really fast and do a midnight loop-the-loop!"

The sleigh began to gather speed
then plunged down from the sky . . .
the stars all shone as Santa Baby
cried out "Fly, Roo, fly!"

But then the sleigh went

bump,

bump,

BUMP!

The two friends gave a shout . . .

. . . As they knocked into a chimney . . . and tumbled all about.
With snow upon his eyelashes and hanging upside down,
Santa Baby howled – he was a long way from the ground.

He dangled from the rooftop
feeling silly, cold and sad,
and called out very miserably,
"PLEASE HELP! I need you, Dad!"

Then suddenly he heard some
jingling bells upon a sleigh.
The whinnying of reindeer
told him help was on its way.

"My daddy's here!" cried Santa Baby, yelling with delight,
and he leapt into his father's arms and squeezed with all his might.

"Perhaps you'd like to tell me
what you're doing out of bed?"
"It's a Present Rescue Mission,
Dad!" Santa Baby said.

Santa, he tried not to laugh
but, no, he wasn't able . . .
"You silly pair," he ho-ho-hoed,
"you should have read the labels."

"These presents are for us!" they squealed. "Whatever can they be?"
Santa gave a merry laugh, "On Christmas Day you'll see!

Now – I think you've both had *quite* enough excitement for one day,
the sun will soon be rising, so hop up into my sleigh!"

The sleigh bells jingled once again as up and off they flew,
and this time Santa Baby's wish . . . it really did come true.
For – higher, higher, higher – Santa's sleigh began to fly,
and – faster, faster, faster – it sped up into the sky.

Till Roo and Santa Baby felt a tingling in their toes,
they held their breath and gave a squeak as up, up, up they rose.
Then suddenly they took a dive and with one great big swoop . . .
Santa's magic Christmas sleigh did one HUGE loop-the-loop!

At home, the two friends yawned
as they were tucked into their beds,
with dreams of their adventures
dancing brightly round their heads.

Sweet dreams of stars and stockings
and a magic snowy night,

of playful elves and penguins
and a midnight moonlit flight.

On Christmas morning Santa Baby opened his surprise.
You'll never guess – a Santa suit in just the perfect size!

And, look – a special Santa scarf made just for Little Roo . . .

"Yippee!" they cried together,
"Next year we're going, too!"

For Mae & Elle xx – S.P-H.

To Ma n Pa with love xx – A.G.

Bloomsbury Publishing, London, Oxford, New Delhi, New York and Sydney

First published in Great Britain in 2015 by Bloomsbury Publishing Plc
50 Bedford Square, London, WC1B 3DP

A CIP catalogue record for this book is available from the British Library

ISBN 978 1 4088 4948 4 (HB)
ISBN 978 1 4088 4949 1 (PB)
ISBN 978 1 4088 4947 7 (eBook)

Printed in China by Leo Paper Products, Heshan, Guangdong

1 3 5 7 9 10 8 6 4 2

www.bloomsbury.com

All papers used by Bloomsbury Publishing are natural, recyclable products
made from wood grown in well-managed forests.
The manufacturing processes conform to the environmental regulations
of the country of origin

BLOOMSBURY is a registered trademark of Bloomsbury Publishing Plc